Withdrawn

For Emma and Tiffany

Text copyright © 1996 by Vivian French
Illustrations copyright © 1996 by John Prater

First U.S. edition 1996

Library of Congress Cataloging-in-Publication Data

Prater, John.
Once upon a picnic / conceived and illustrated by John Prater ;
text by Vivian French.—1st U.S. ed.
Summary: While Mom and Dad do nothing but daydream at the
picnic, the young boy keeps very active noticing all kinds of things
going on around them. ISBN 1-56402-810-0 (alk. paper)
[1. Picnicking—Fiction. 2. Characters and characteristics in literature—
Fiction. 3. Stories in rhyme.] I. French, Vivian. II. Title.
PZ8.3.P8501   1996
[E]—dc20   95-19912

10 9 8 7 6 5 4 3 2 1

Printed in Hong Kong

This book was typeset in ITC Garamond Book.
The pictures were done in watercolor.

Candlewick Press
2067 Massachusetts Avenue
Cambridge, Massachusetts 02140

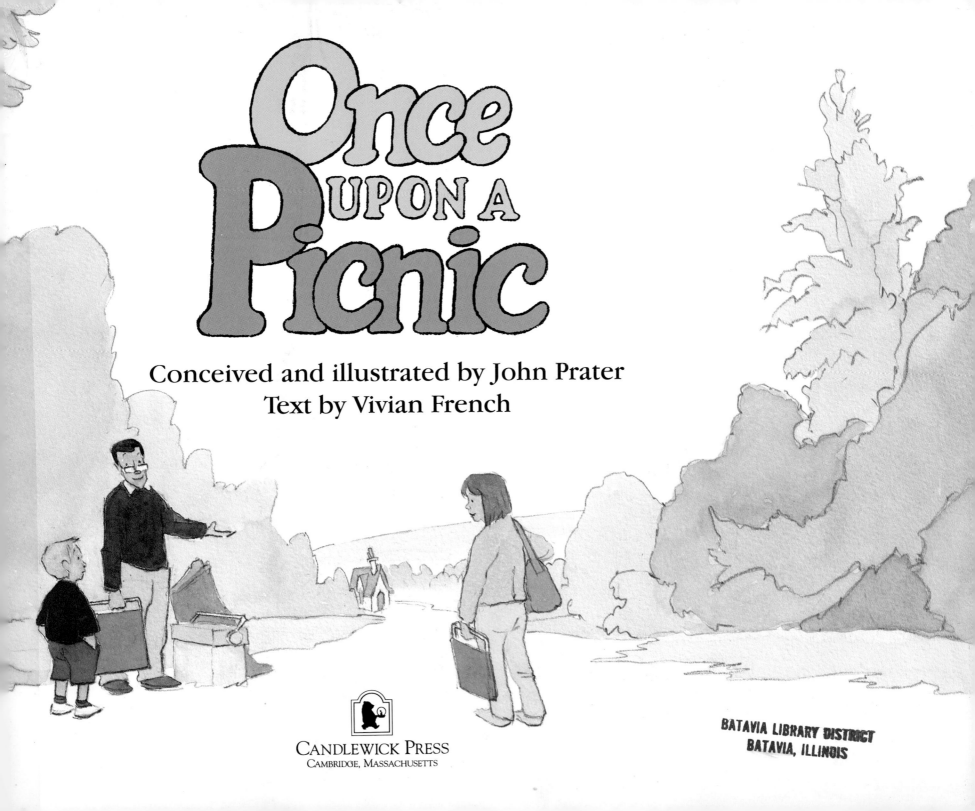

Once Upon a Picnic

Conceived and illustrated by John Prater
Text by Vivian French

CANDLEWICK PRESS
CAMBRIDGE, MASSACHUSETTS

Out on a picnic,
Mom, Dad, and me.
Not much to do,
not much to see.

Mom is setting
up her chair.
Here come
the three bears.

Mom and Dad
just sit and dream.
Is that a troll
beside the stream?

Nothing much
for me to do.
Who's that little girl
talking to?

Now I'm hungry . . .
What's in here?
Apples, cookies,
and root beer.

That kite's high
above the ground.
What's that giant
stomping sound?

Run! Run!
As fast as you can!
Run and play,
you gingerbread man!

Mr. Wolf is
by the trees.
That girl's flowers
made him sneeze!

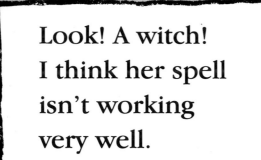

Look! A witch!
I think her spell
isn't working
very well.

All those children
in that shoe.
Look how much
they have to do!

We've been sitting
here all day . . .
Little bear
might like to play.

Playing ball
is so much fun.
Come back, come back,
everyone!